MILDRED
and
SAM
and Their Babies

by Sharleen Collicott

LAURA GERINGER BOOKS

An Imprint of HarperCollins*Publishers*

To Sharon and Chuck Ferges
and their big "babies":
Doug, Michael, and Steven
—S.C.

HarperCollins®, 🐭®, and I Can Read Book®
are trademarks of HarperCollins Publishers Inc.

Mildred and Sam and Their Babies
Copyright © 2005 by Sharleen Collicott

Library of Congress Cataloging-in-Publication Data
Collicott, Sharleen.
    Mildred and Sam and their babies / by Sharleen Collicott. — 1st ed.
        p.   cm. (An I can read book)
    Level 2.
    Summary: Mildred and Sam's eight baby mice prepare for their first day of school.
    ISBN 0-06-058111-5 — ISBN 0-06-058112-3 (lib. bdg.)
    [1. Mice—Fiction.   2. Family life—Fiction.   3. Worry—Fiction.   4. First day of school—
Fiction.   5. Schools—Fiction.]   I. Title.   II. Series.
PZ7.C67758Mk   2005   2003024245
[E]—dc22   CIP
                                                                                      AC

1   2   3   4   5   6   7   8   9   10
❖
First Edition

CONTENTS

LITTLE MOUSE DREAMS

Mildred and Sam had eight baby mice.

Each day

the babies grew bigger and bigger.

Sam liked to play outside with them.

Mildred liked to worry.

"Our babies need something new,"

Sam said.

"Something new?" Mildred asked.

"Don't worry," Sam said.

"Our babies will be just fine."

The next day Mildred and Sam

went for a walk with their babies.

"The sun is too bright," Mildred said.

"The babies are wearing bonnets,"

Sam answered.

"The buggy goes too fast," Mildred said.

"Don't worry," Sam said.

"Our babies will be just fine."

That night the babies dreamed

they were buggy racing

down a steep hill.

"Faster, faster!" the babies shouted.

They passed a bunny rabbit.

"Hello, Bunny Rabbit," the babies said.

"Tell us about the trees in the forest."

But before the rabbit could answer,

Mildred and Sam came

and took their babies home.

The next day Mildred and Sam

took their babies on the swings.

"The seats don't look strong enough,"

Mildred said.

"I made them out of daffodil leaves,"

Sam answered.

"The swings go too high," Mildred said.

"Don't worry," Sam said.

"Our babies will be just fine."

That night the babies dreamed

they were swinging high into the sky.

"Higher, higher!" the babies shouted.

They soared up to the moon.

"Hello, Moon," the babies said.

"Tell us about the stars in the sky."

But before the moon could answer,

Mildred and Sam came

and took their babies home.

The next day Mildred and Sam

took the babies to the pond.

"It is too cold for swimming,"

Mildred said.

"But the water is warm," Sam answered.

"The water is too rough," Mildred said.

"Don't worry," Sam said.

"Our babies will be just fine."

That night the babies dreamed

they were swimming in the pond.

"Splash, splash!" the babies shouted.

They floated down a waterfall.

"Hello, Yellow Frog," the babies said.

"Tell us about the fish in the pond."

But before the yellow frog

could answer,

Mildred and Sam came

and took their babies home.

The next day Mildred and Sam

made their babies breakfast.

"Oatmeal is too messy," Mildred said.

"The babies will use napkins,"

Sam answered.

"The fruit is not ripe enough,"

Mildred said.

"Don't worry," Sam said.

"Everything will be just fine."

That night the babies dreamed

they were eating a great feast.

"More, more!" the babies shouted.

The table was covered

with cakes and cookies.

"Hello, Gingerbread Man,"

the babies said.

"Tell us how you got to be so sweet."

But before the gingerbread man

could answer,

Mildred and Sam came

and took their babies home.

The next day Mildred and Sam

gave their babies a bath in a wooden tub.

"The water is too hot," Mildred said.

"Baths are supposed to be warm,"

Sam answered.

"There are too many bubbles,"

Mildred said.

"Don't worry," Sam said.

"Everything will be just fine."

That night the babies dreamed

they were sailing in a boat.

"Sail on, sail on!" the babies shouted.

A pirate ship approached.

"Hello, Pirates," the babies said.

"Tell us about your treasure."

But before the pirates could answer,

Mildred and Sam came

and took their babies home.

The next day Mildred and Sam

had lunch together in their garden.

"I think our babies

are ready for something new," Sam said.

"Something new?" Mildred asked.

"Don't worry," Sam said.

"Our babies will be just fine."

28

SOMETHING NEW

Many weeks went by.

Mildred and Sam's eight baby mice

had grown bigger and bigger.

Sam allowed the babies

to play outside by themselves.

Mildred still worried.

Sam built eight scooters

and put baskets on the front.

The babies learned how to ride.

Mildred made colorful backpacks.

The babies tried them on for size.

Sam taught the babies

to tie their shoelaces.

The babies tied ribbons

in Mildred's fur.

Mildred knitted hats and sweaters.

The babies dressed themselves.

Sam sharpened pencils

and drew pictures

on brown paper lunch bags.

The babies put desserts inside.

Soon the babies were ready

for the first day of school.

They weren't really babies anymore.

Mildred and Sam led their children

down the path to the schoolhouse.

"Are you sure they're ready?"

Mildred asked.

"Don't worry," Sam said.

46

And the babies were just fine.